To all my amazing children in class 4C. I couldn't ask for a better class on my first full time position. Hope you enjoy the novel.

2

Curiosity

Mrs Rainbow stood in front of the stage six children, wishing them all the best of luck, as they prepared to move onto their new high schools. "Now children you have been with us for seven incredible years and I would like to thank you for all your hard work and dedication. We have yet again reached the end of another academic year where we all have to say our goodbyes".

It was at this point that the parents, at the back of the room, began to cry more heavily than just the odd sobs from half an hour previously.

"Now remember that as you take your well-earned final gift, no one should ever talk about the gift that you have received here today to anyone under age, unless they choose to give up their gift for the rest of their lives. You know this well, as you have each received a gift each year for the last five stages. Our past history has taught us not to take anything for granted. That is why we earn our gifts each year. Do you all accept these rules?"

The year six children agreed nervously and awaited their sixth and final gift.

Mrs Rainbow stood back a little "This will come as a shock to the system but, my oh my, I'm sure you will agree that this is the best gift of all time". As the head teacher finished what seemed like her final words, the year six children began very slowly to let the others in the room hear their first impression of the gift they had already started receiving.

"Oooohs" and "ahhhhhs" swept around the front of the hall as, one by one, the children at the front of the assembly hall began to look at everyone and everything so curiously around the great sized room. Eyes grew wide, as a stunned set of children looked at each other excitedly. Curiosity at the beginning of the afternoon assembly, turned into wide spread joy and excitement.

"Something tells me that this summer will be one to remember" exclaimed Mrs Rainbow. "Before you know it, our new children starting school will be standing here receiving their leaver's gift. Time will fly. If parents and their children wish to walk around school one final time before they leave this afternoon I would encourage you to do so".

Little Millie, who was one of the children just starting her journey through stage one, looked up in awe and wonder. What was the gift the children in year six had been given? What was happening? What were they staring at?

Stage 1.Miss Bell and the gifts of ...

Summer soon passed as Millie and all the other new children began their school life with Miss Bell. The usual daily routine encouraged all the children to learn to share and get along with each other. This didn't seem to be any kind of problem for Millie who settled into school really well. Millie was a quiet girl who seemed happy to do just about anything. She was an average height for her age and wore what any typical little girl would wear as her uniform for the start of school. To say that Millie was a quiet girl wasn't quite true as really she didn't speak at all. This was the same as Daisy Mae who quickly became great friends with Millie. They would share most toys and things that were available in the classroom while always choosing the same option as each other on the choosing chart each morning.

Part of Millie's school routine, in Miss Bell's class, was to go to the choosing chart every morning. On the wall the chart had lots of choices to pick from including sticking the word 'in' or 'out' to their chart if they had arrived in school: like a do it yourself register. It was then made up of four choices. The first choice was to pick an activity from the English section. This was one of Millie's favourites. Usually the choices were the same each day. The children could explore writing by typing on the computer. Some chose to visit the role play area which was currently a space theme. Some children had to spell their name working with Miss Bell on a whiteboard, while some picked their own reading book and tried their best to copy some words of their own. Although there were lots of choices, the children only ever had time to pick one.

Millie and Daisy -Mae would usually race over to the choosing board and pick the role play area if they could. On this particular morning the girls had to share the moon decorated corner with Dexter and Tony (everyone called him TJ). The role play corner was covered in many grey shades for the Earth's moon. All four children would flick through the pictures of space trying to learn as much as they could remember, while pretending to be astronauts in their bright white spacesuits.

Next, was picking a task from the second section, which was Maths.

Daisy- Mae and Millie would always want to work together whenever they could. Millie enjoyed counting and learning her numbers up to twenty. She would very often write them down and take them to her teacher. Miss Bell would look rather pleased and do the usual thing that she always did, which was to bend down and give a gentle hug to all her children every time they did something really well. Millie and Daisy Mae would be very happy with themselves, especially while in the background Lily C was trying to pull her finger out of the shopping till, who had trapped it in there after trying to give Alexis her change. To make matters even more confusing, Alexis was buying her own stuffed cuddly toy wolf back that had been abducted early in the morning by Ellis.

Lunchtime arrived and all the children from Miss Bell's class would walk in to the school dining hall in a very haphazard manner. Everyone would be given a dinner. Each day the children ate their lunch provided by the dinner lady Mrs Howard without complaints. It seemed everyone was happy each and every day. Food was food to Millie, even if Ellis could munch it down whether it was lumpy, chewy or soggy. When the children in Millie's class sat down they couldn't help but notice that the children of the next two older classes were always moving their mouths and were excited every time it came to lunch. They couldn't understand why, especially when the food was mostly the same every day.

As the afternoon started, next on the choosing chart for Millie was to take part in something sporty outside. Each day Miss Bell, early in the morning, would set up a sports activity in the outside area. Coming up soon was sports day, so Miss Bell had left six spoons and six sponge rubber balls so the children could practise the egg and spoon race. Millie had enjoyed the afternoon's races with Tyler, Bradley, Justin and Natasha. They all really loved their sports and hated losing. As Millie stood waiting for one of her races, she couldn't help but notice a boy in stage six who had been told to stand on the inside of the cone during a game of Rounder's. Not only did the boy not understand but two minutes later he approached Mr Brown, the stage six teacher, saying that he couldn't get his feet inside the cone as they were too big. Millie looked confused by the whole situation.

Once another break time had passed by, this time with its grey skies, the children began their final choice from their choosing chart. Millie had chosen junk modelling. The theme this week would be like the role play corner – space. Instructions using black and white pictures were left on the table. This showed the children how to build a rocket ship. She had worked with Harrison throughout the final part of the day. They both looked at each other and noticed that Chloe B had glued just as many art pieces on to her body as her actual rocket. Harrison thought that she might take off!

Anytime a child in the class achieved something worth noticing, Miss Bell would always be the first to kneel down and give them a cuddle to show her delight. Once the end of the day would arrive Miss Bell would always finish in her classroom by letting the children take a well-earned sleep. Everyone would pull a little sleeping bag out at the end of the day.

Later, Millie would take her rocket home and put it on her shelf in her bedroom.

This pattern of play and development would continue throughout the year with Millie and Daisy - Mae keen to please their teacher. Time would soon pass.

The excitement was building up in school as this week would be the end of their first school stage. A year had already passed for Millie and the other children in Miss Bell's class. The leavers were getting ready to receive their final gift in the school hall, before everyone moved on one more stage.

The morning of the leaver's assembly arrived but before everyone was asked to go to the school hall, Miss Bell had sat her class down for one last time on her carpet. She asked them to rest just like they would normally do in the afternoon, inside their sleeping bags. What the children didn't know was that a special gift was about to be given to each of them, their first gift ever.

"Wake up children!" said Miss Bell in a quiet but cheery and excited voice "It's time to get up". There was a sudden shock that something just then had happened for the very first time ever.

 "I know this maybe surprising children but as you have reached the end of stage one, you will now receive your first ever gift from school, which shows that you have grown up enough to move to the second stage". The children looked on astonished. In all the time they had spent with Miss Bell, no one had ever heard her speak or themselves for that matter. This was particularly surprising as no child in stage one had ever noticed that something was different to start with.

Miss Bell continued. "In previous years, not everyone appreciated the gifts that we were brought up with. Our leaders of our new world have decided to make us look after each gift as we receive it.

As you children get older you will be given more gifts. At the end of the first stage you are rewarded with the gift of speech and sound which is why you can hear my voice for the very first time. You should now be able to talk to your friends and others for the very first time while also being able to listen. I know this feels scary but try to use your voice now. You will have already heard so much in this first couple of minutes".

Slowly, the room filled with unknown voices coming from very familiar faces. Millie looked amazed as she sat up next to Daisy –Mae.

 "Hi I'm Millie"

"Hi. I'm Daisy - Mae"

The children were shocked and astonished. All through the year the children had looked at books together, explored objects together and been creative together but now it was like the whole world had changed. Miss Bell spoke again. "Years ago children would have been able to try to speak and listen from birth, but now the brain stores all the sounds and words up ready for you to use them when we decide you are ready".

The noises seemed weirdly odd and for a while it almost seemed painful to be given this skill as so many children were experimenting with their words and sounds. Miss Bell had let her class enjoy this first stage as long as possible before asking the children to line up at the door, something she had not been able to do before.

"This afternoon we will go into assembly where our stage six children will receive their final gift from school".

Millie immediately remembered a year ago, back to when she wondered what on earth the older children were staring at in the hall. She desperately wanted to know.

"You see children" exclaimed Miss Bell, "each year as you grow up through school, each of you will receive a gift in each stage. Six classrooms. Six stages. Six gifts. When you leave you will receive the best gift of all. Finally, the most important rule of all is to never mention your gift to anyone under your age. If you give the secret away then you will lose your gift permanently".

As the children came to terms with what had just happened to them, the noises of tired stretching children and the early stages of excitement began to spread across the room. Not only was this going to be the best summer ever, but there were still five more gifts to come. Millie and Daisy – Mae started to talk. The conversation finished with Millie asking "I wonder what the other gifts will be?"

Stage 2. Mr Baker and the gifts of …

Summer had gone so quickly for all the children but each had developed their language and listening skills in their own unique way. Although Millie had loved both gifts, the listening gift was her favourite. She had heard her mother and father for the first time and was surprised by the sounds of their voices. Mum's voice seemed almost screechy to dad's whose voice sounded a lot lower. It was because of this fact, that Millie really appreciated the gifts and naturally wanted to explore them further.

While visiting her uncle, Millie had been described as sounding exactly the way he had imagined.

"Uncle Mikey?" quizzed Millie, "Who is in charge of giving the gifts out? Is it just teachers?"

Uncle Mikey took a deep breath and began to explain. "One of the first questions that are asked is, who is in charge? It was decided a long time ago that the things we take for granted like speaking and listening was being used wrongly in a world that was being brought up badly. Many years ago our leaders decided that the educators of our future should be allowed to give out the 'gifts' when they thought the time was right, to make sure we don't take anything for granted. Anyway, you don't need to worry about anything like that, so just you enjoy using your gifts. Come on it's time to go".

Today was a special day out in the summer holidays that Millie was definitely looking forward to. Upon hearing the car start its engine for the first time and accelerate from her house, she began to realise how noisy each little street was. There were birds chirping away, the odd dog barking, while the bell from a distant bicycle could be heard. Millie had thought these noises were loud until they reached the city centre. There were so many cars which added to a dreadful collection of noise and chaos. Millie didn't like it at first but eventually grew to like it a little bit later. Finally they had reached their destination of the local zoo.

You can imagine the noises Millie heard for the first time (with mum and dad paying attention to every face Millie would make) as she discovered what sounds each animal made. Penguins, giraffes, elephants, lions, tigers and all the others, Millie was so excited to get back to school to talk to all her friends.

All the children told similar tales of how they used their new 'gifts' over the summer. After all, they had heard and spoken so many new things but hardly had any time to listen to each other since school had finished for the summer.

Miss Bell had a high cheery voice that suited a stage one teacher. Mr Baker though, as he came through the door, was different altogether. His voice was deep and now and again made you jump if he caught you out. However if you did as you were told he was more than fair.

"Welcome to stage two. I trust you have all had fun using your first gifts from stage one?" The children murmured excitedly. "Well now we are back at school, we will be teaching you how to use your speech at the most appropriate time, won't we Taylor and Danny? (They had been caught talking at the back of the room). We will also be teaching you to listen to instructions very carefully indeed and to know when to use your skills at the right time."

The first half of the year with Mr Baker seemed pretty straight forward. He would ask the children to keep exploring their speaking and listening skills further while applying them into the challenges ahead. Mr Baker would teach from new books that the children had never seen before. Each day he would try to catch the children out by asking them to read next or read from a book using a character voice. The children developed their listening and speaking skills more and more as Christmas approached fast.

One week from Christmas the children were given a set of instructions and a batch of cooking ingredients. Mr Baker wanted them to make some food by following a recipe. Working in twos, the children began, what felt like, a long afternoon of hard work. After all, making chocolate cornflake cakes was the hardest dish to make ever. Mr Baker had set up a small cooker in the corner of the classroom. He had put some chocolate on the hob to melt, ready to show in his demonstration. Round and round the room he went coming out with all sorts of comments.

"Brilliant! Brilliant! Brilliant! Brilliant! Well done Finley and George. You have followed the instructions perfectly". The whole room seemed to be looking now. He couldn't praise them enough.

"Archie and Brodie, What are you doing?" It was at this point that the pair of them seemed to have eaten all of the chocolate and left nowhere near enough for the cornflakes.

 "Which one of you decided that it would be a good idea to eat everything before we finished?" Even though both boys were covered in chocolate all around their mouths, they still both pointed to each other at the same time saying they hadn't done anything.

"Never mind" said Mr Baker shaking his head very slowly from side to side.

All of a sudden, one of the children had their hand in the air. "Sir what is that?" the child's hand pointing towards the cooker. Mr Baker had forgotten all about his chocolate warming up. "Quick move out of the way before it sets the ..." It was too late. The next thing to be heard was a sound so loud and mighty that all the stage two children immediately covered their ears up as they had never experienced anything like it".

The siren wailed for what seemed like hours. Mr Baker thought he was going to be sacked after he had completely ruined the chocolate and a new cooking pan. The smoke had only filled a small part of the ceiling but clearly it was enough to set off the fire alarm.

After everyone had evacuated the school and been accounted for, everyone went back to class. Mrs Rainbow the school head teacher walked in just behind Mr Baker.

"I'm so sorry Mrs Rainbow" pleaded Mr Baker "I promise nothing like this will ever happen again". Mrs Rainbow walked over to where the mess had been created.

"It just so happens Mr Baker, that your little accident in here actually never started the fire alarm" exclaimed Mrs Rainbow. "In fact a very naughty boy by the name of Garvey in stage five had decided against all temptation to push the fire alarm button on the way past. He will now, of course, lose one of his 'gifts'. Am I right in saying that the children in this classroom would never do anything like that would they?"

All the children replied "No Mrs Rainbow".

The head teacher had one more look up and down the classroom before leaving with strict words for Mr Baker which went somewhere along the lines of "Don't let it happen again" followed by "I think that this would be an appropriate time now Mr Baker, especially the safety aspect". Mr Baker asked the children to sit down as the next part of the lesson would be the most important of the year.

"Mrs Rainbow and I have decided, as usual at this time of the year, to allow our stage two children to receive their next gift". All the children looked extremely excited. "You have all worked incredibly hard and I hope you enjoy the next reward". Mr Baker turned to stand at the front of the room as the children began to experience the most unusual sensation ever.

"Errr. That's not nice at all" beamed Ashton from the middle of the room.

"That is the smell of something burnt" replied Mr Baker.

"Smell?" queried Ashton. "What's a smell?"

"Something that your nose is used for. Some things smell pleasant and some things smell horrible" explained Mr Baker. "Better still, why don't you try eating some of the chocolate that we melted this afternoon. I'm sure you'll enjoy that".

He wasn't wrong. The children began licking and tasting every bowl of chocolate in the room like they had never eaten food before. But there was something so different this time from all the other food they had ever eaten.

"Taste boys and girls. Taste" said Mr Baker "Your stage two rewards are the gifts of smelling and tasting". Mr Baker introduced the new skills with the biggest smile in the world on his face.

"How come we get our gift in the middle of the year?" asked Amelia.

"Coming up, is a time where the teachers think it is best to give you your first delicious, tasty and sumptuous smelling turkey dinner. I can't wait for you to pull some amusing faces" said Mr Baker mischievously.

Sure enough, on the last day of the Christmas term, the children, led by Mr Baker, were marched into the school dining hall where a table of silver trays awaited them. The dinnertime staff came along and lifted the lids of the trays. The intense smells that came off the trays straight away was enough to get the children's' mouths watering and full with saliva for the very first time in their lives.

Each child was given a sample of each food from the Christmas dinner. A fluffy splodge of creamy and buttery mashed potatoes, sliced carrots, a mixture of steaming cauliflower and broccoli and a stuffing ball. Next was a food where the outside was crispy and the inside was fluffy known as a roast potato with a final food that was to be a surprise. All of this was to be covered in turkey flavoured gravy.

Each child began to taste and smell their food. The faces that the children pulled ranged from pure delight and tastiness to scrunched up and looking at the school dining staff and Mr Baker, like they had deliberately tried to poison their own children. It was especially funny when they had put the secret food in their mouths at the same time and had discovered it was something known as a brussel sprout.

The children were full from their dinner and suddenly a few questions started to be asked.

"Mr Baker. Are there other foods for us to learn about?" enquired Justin.

"Yeah or to taste and smell?" asked Sophie.

"There are millions of foods all over our world for you to try and taste and smell. No doubt at home you will experience new foods as well as time goes on. Some of them you will like and some of them you will not" explained Mr Baker.

It was at this point that Millie noticed something strange. She had glanced over to the other side of the dining hall where the new stage one children were being asked to sit. She realised that the children in stage one had no talking skills yet or the ability to listen. Yet here Millie was, with her second stage gifts of smelling and tasting. Part of her wanted to go over and tell the stage one children what was about to happen to them but then she remembered that they couldn't hear her anyway. She also remembered what the school had always said about children who break the rules- you will lose one of your 'gifts' - which in Millie's eyes was not worth risking. More great cooking experiences took place as the year progressed and by the time the gift of smelling and tasting had become part of the children's normal daily routine, Millie started to think about what unusual 'gifts' might be coming up in stage three.

Stage 3. Mrs Story and the gifts of ...

Mrs Story was a strict teacher but fair. The year would start simply by writing down sentences and making sure, as ever, that they made sense and included capital letters, full stops with beautiful handwriting. Maths was all about making sure each child's adding, subtracting, dividing and multiplication was correct. It seemed that all Mrs Story was interested in was getting the simple things right. Every day they carried out the same things over and over. Millie liked Mrs Story but found her lessons very boring.

"The more practice we put into our sentences, the better writers we will be later on" explained the stage three teacher. All the children sat there waiting for something interesting but it never came. After break the same routine happened with Maths. They would learn their times tables and solving basic calculations. Millie would have to agree though that she did know her times tables extremely well.

The end of September arrived. Only one month into stage three and it already felt like the same length in time as stage one and two combined and multiplied by 10. (This was the best way of describing how Millie felt, especially when they had been multiplying by ten that very morning)!

The next day came. Mrs Story asked her writers to take out their pencils. The children sat there almost lifeless.

"Now, now children" said Mrs Story concerned "If we continue to write with a lack of imagination then our stories and poems will be most dull".

"What's an imagination?" quizzed Harrison.

"You will find out very soon Harrison. As will everyone in the room" said Mrs Story very giddily.

The children sat up very quickly in their chairs and looked as though they were ready to learn immediately.

"Today children, I would like you to write down a story or poem of your choice" instructed Mrs Story "it can be as long or as short as it needs to be, remembering of course, that it must have its capital letters, full stops, beautiful handwriting and most importantly of all, it makes sense".

"How are we going to do that? asked Katy confused "when we haven't been taught how to write stories or poems"

"Just try please" replied Mrs Story "and see how you get on".

The children looked really confused and puzzled about what to do. They started to write as best they could but by the look of the whole room, nothing really seemed to be going well at all.

"Is there a problem?" asked Mrs Story.

Katy put her hand up. "Mrs Story, I don't know how to write a story or poem. Please can you help?"

With a big smile Mrs Story stood up at her desk near the front of the classroom and spoke firmly. "Of course. Who else in my class would like help?" Suddenly the entire class put their hands up. "Why didn't you say so?" said Mrs Story in a confident mood. "Here are your stage three gifts children. Enjoy and use them wisely". Excitedly, Millie and all her class friends attentively awaited a most unexpected moment to happen. All of a sudden, Millie's brain started to reach thoughts from deep within her own head. Using past memories and things she had learnt about, she was changing the names and ideas to make new creative ideas of her own. All the children began to wonder about everyone and everything from A to Z.

"This is always the problem every year" spoke Mrs Story. Clapping as loudly as she could, she shouted "Children! Children! Children! Stop day dreaming!"

Millie tried to focus but found it really difficult to control so many of these, whatever they were called, going on inside her head.

Daisy Mae turned to her friend Millie. "What's this gift called?" Millie shrugged her shoulders and then put her hand in the air.

"Yes Millie?"

"Mrs Story what exactly is this gift?" asked Millie enquiringly.

"My dear did you not hear me before? I have given you the gift of imagination and problem solving. You will be able to write and tell great stories with terrific detail, write and tell your own imaginative poetry as well as apply all those numbers from Maths in to difficult word problems and calculations. Children we have work to do". Just like that, the stage three gifts weren't given at the end of the year or the middle, but these, at the start of the school year.

Millie, all of a sudden, loved being in Mrs Story's class. However, one person in particular that seemed to be flying with his Maths, was Robert. There wasn't any question he couldn't answer for his own age group or probably the year above. If any areas of Maths were his favourites, it would be statistics and fractions. Just yesterday, while everyone in the room sat in perfect silence, as they couldn't give an answer to two thirds add three fifths multiplied by 0, Robert very calmly raised his hand and said 0. Mrs Story was delighted. She was even more delighted with her two star pupils Hayley and Chloe who were writing fantastic pieces of work each and every day. In fact by the end of the year, all the children had made such great progress, that Mrs Story allowed the children to pick out their favourite piece of writing and read it out to the class. Hayley and Chloe had produced a stunning poem about a wobbly donkey which read as follows:

This is a tale of Wobbly Donkey,

who works on Blackpool sands.

Who plods from the Pier to the Tower,

arriving wobbly on the hour.

His friends are Daisy, Dippy and Danny,

Donald, Donna and Troy.

and their owner is an elderly
gentleman

who goes by the name of Roy.

Each day the donkeys walk all in a
line,

to the stables on the edge of the
town.

Where they all get wrapped up for a
good night's sleep,

each in their own little special gown.

One night, bad weather arrived

and Wobbly Donkey was being
called names.

All the other donkeys teased him
about his legs

that clearly weren't the same.

"You're a freak", "You're a joke" they said,

"You're holding all of us back"

Just then lightning struck the stable

And gave the door, a great big crack.

Wobbly Donkey, feeling sad, grabbed his things

and pushed his way through the door.

Out into the big wide world

where he hoped for something more.

This is Wobbly Donkey,

Who trudges along the sand.

Who tried to play the symbols,

for his local big brass band.

But when he crashed his arms
together,

he discovered something wrong.

His arms were different sizes,

and so he wrecked the beautiful
songs.

He decided to solve the problem,

and set out to find a cure.

Should he make one leg longer? Or
the others shorter?

He wasn't sure.

But one thing is for certain,

I'm sure you will agree.

That unless donkey does something,

A Wobbly Donkey he will be.

He found his local doctor,

who agreed to try and help.

So he reached for the bottles of medicine,

that were lying on the top of the shelf.

Take one of these tablets, read bottle one,

and your leg is sure to grow.

But mix it up with bottle two,

the opposite will happen you know.

The doctor grabbed both bottles,

his eye sight wasn't the best.

He gave a tablet to Wobbly,

and thought he'd given it for the best.

But soon we all discovered,

there must've been a mistake.

Wobbly Donkey's legs were wider apart,

And were nearly about to break.

In panic and desperation the doctor sprang to life.

He pulled out his mobile phone and rang up his intelligent wife.

"I've made a mistake, I've made a mistake. I don't know what to do".

"Calm down. Calm down" replied his wife "I've got the solution for you".

"In 4 hours' time give Wobbly a tablet

from the other bottle my dear".

"So that his legs start to close together again,

not putting everyone through fear".

So finally things went back to how they were

at the start of this rhyme.

Which means that Wobbly Donkey, is still a Wobbly Donkey

at this present time.

This is Wobbly Donkey,

walking in zig-zag fashion.

With his head down low and feeling glum,

Without hardly any passion.

He tried the doctor, he tried the medicine,

But his legs were all just the same.

Maybe all the other donkeys were definitely right,

To call him all those names.

Meanwhile back at the stables,

Roy was all in shock.

"Someone's stolen Wobbly

and he's brilliant at his job".

Daisy, Dippy, Danny, Donald, Donna and Troy,

hung their donkey heads in shame.

They saw how upset their owner was,

and knew they were to blame.

Wobbly by now had stumbled out of town,

all on his lonesome own.

Wishing that his legs had grown the same,

from the day he was first born.

Wobbly was annoyed with his stable friends,

and knew that trudging away wasn't right.

He needed to stand his ground tonight

and put up a bit of a fight.

He turned himself round and began to march back,

To where he knew he belonged.

Reaching the stables and all his friends at midnight,

as the bell tower gonged.

"Wobbly you're back" shouted Danny,

the others were all delighted.

As was Roy in the morning,

when it was the first thing that he sighted.

While Wobbly was away,

The other donkeys explained what had taken place.

That Wobbly was the star attraction

as the customers missed his wobbly legs and his gorgeous face.

Roy the owner began to walk them all,

on their usual trip,

From Blackpool Tower to Central Pier

without losing his grip.

Wobbly was happy and so were the others

and the owner was paying his way.

The donkeys were locked up safe and sound,

Sleeping in the hay.

The lesson of the poem is not to be mean,

Stay individual and be mentally strong.

Be kind and act like Wobbly Donkey

So you can't be far from wrong.

Mrs Story cried just like she did when she had read it out to the class for the first time earlier in the year. "That is definitely the gift of imagination and we have some fine mathematicians in this room. Now my children you are ready for Mr Church - Hill in stage four". In a flash, after working hard on training the imagination and applying numbers into everyday life, summer had arrived again. It was hard to believe that stage three had come to an end.

Stage 4. Mr Church – Hill and the gift of...

It was hard for the children to imagine a world now, without the ability to talk, the ability to listen, smell, taste, solve problems or use their imaginations. This summer had been organised. A mixture of playing games because Millie could and then some more studying from her own mum who thought it would be a good idea to keep her learning about new things. Even though Millie had imagined new games and played them for the first time, there were still moments that would surprise her out of nowhere. New tastes at lunch and dinner time and new sounds never previously heard, were all part of the surprises greeting her in everyday life. Each time something new was discovered, the children would share their experiences and discuss it deeply. Entering stage four, all of a sudden, had the children guessing what skills or thing they might be introduced to next. Curiosity was at an all-time high, especially now one of their gifts was the gift of imagination.

Mr Church – Hill was probably one of the oldest teachers in school. He often joked that if he had never left school, he would be entering stage fifty five by now, thus prompting half of the class to work his age out, while the other half waited for the answer to be given to them on a plate.

"Never mind my age" interrupted Mr Church – Hill "stage four I promise you, will be one of the hardest stages you have ever had to get through".

Normally, each child would take the challenge of a new gift without thinking about it because in the past they had no choice but to accept it. However, they had now been introduced to a developing imagination that would often run wild and send most children into a day dream. Staying focussed throughout Mr Church – Hill's stage was going to be extremely difficult.

"Who has enjoyed their gifts so far as they have gone through school?" asked the stage four teacher without really looking at the children's hands in the air.

"Have you ever thought about why we give the gifts out? Or why we give them to you at the time that we do? Have you ever thought about when the gifts come to an end?" said Mr Church – Hill.

The children sat attentively. Millie had thought about all those questions before but each time she asked someone at home, she was always greeted with the same answer of "they will tell you at school when the time is right".

"Have you always had the answer - they will tell you at school when they're ready?" asked Mr Church – Hill. The children started to nod up and down and call out.

Ethan stood up and shouted "Yeah that's the answer I always get". It seemed everyone was going through the same stage of thinking which made Millie feel a lot better.

Mr Church – Hill stood in front of the children with a serious face. It wasn't as though any other teacher hadn't been serious, but at this moment it seemed as though something important was about to be explained.

Mr Church – Hill explained that "In the past, human behaviour has not been the best. In the not too distant past the Earth had been through what was described as the final world war. All corners of the earth were arguing and fighting. When the final war came to an end, there was so much damage, that we formed our new leaders for this area and decided to start again keeping all the technology we had discovered, but improve our behaviour and appreciation for the things we always took for granted. It was decided that trustworthy community members would be in charge of making decisions that would be in the best interest of the area. The leaders decided that teachers would introduce certain gifts as children grew up in school. That is why teachers were chosen to pass on these gifts"

"What if people didn't want that to happen?" asked Norman looking really concerned.

"Well not everybody did agree. Eventually some people moved out of the area to live in different parts of the Earth. Those that chose to stay decided to make a fresh start and live by the new rules of our leaders. It is my job to teach you about all those 'mistakes' of the past and get you ready for your stage four gift but I warn you it will not be easy. You will experience something that you have never experienced before."

The autumn and winter terms went by and Mr Church – Hill looked at world war one and two in great detail. The children had a really good knowledge of both major events and the stage four teacher was more than happy to move onto his final terms work. However, although the children had looked at both wars in a vast amount of detail, the children sat quietly and imagined what life used to be like, inspired by all the photographs in old books.

The summer term began and first up was to look at the final world war. Mr Church – Hill explained how people took advantage of others to try and gain for their own personal wealth and that it would happen on small and big scales. People would die on the other side of the world without others even caring. Jealous people would try to live their lives better than others, almost like it was a competition to do so. Along the way we would pollute our own planet while also not caring whether or not animals would survive or become extinct.

The children watched a video clip of their own planet being destroyed slowly and painfully. It didn't seem like this could be true as their school was so wonderful. The video came to an end showing the devastating effects of world war three with Millie and all the other children sitting down absorbing all the information they could. They had never seen anything like this before which was exactly what Mr Church – Hill had said would happen.

"We are going to watch the video again children. As we go through the video a second time, you will begin to experience something unlike anything you have ever experienced before. This will be exceptionally hard for some of you, if not all of you, in the room".

At this point, the children in the room were looking rather calm and ready to learn about more facts of the previous world war when Millie all of a sudden, held her stomach like she was ill or about to be sick. The same thing started to spread, like a wild fire, right around the classroom of stage four.

"This is the first stage of your new gift" explained Mr Church – Hill moving around the room looking at each child worriedly.

"I don't like it" called Finley from the front of the room.

Slowly, all the children around the room looked at each other not knowing how to describe what was happening to them. Some children seemed to be looking more calm than others. Why was that so? Why was Millie holding her stomach really tightly?

Immediately Mr Church – Hill shouted. "Stop!" The whole room came to a complete silence. The children looked at each other, as if to say, did you just take part in what I took part in?

Mr Church – Hill was going to ask the children if they had enjoyed the video clip but he hadn't even started the recording yet. Instead he asked if the children liked what the start of their new gift was. No one in the room put a hand in the air. Whatever this was, not one child liked it or wanted to be part of it. The information about all the world wars was enough to make everyone react in their own way.

"That, children" while Mr Church – Hill walked around the room, "is the gift of emotions or more specifically the darker emotions of nervousness, worry, being upset and crying". Mr Church – Hill had now stopped in front of Kiera. He wiped away what seemed like drops of water dribbling down or resting upon her face. "I said that this would be difficult children. I notice Millie that you are holding your stomach still like some of the others in the room. That is what we call a gut reaction or a nervousness for what is about to happen. Did you all of a sudden feel like you were worried about what was coming up?"

Millie nodded her head, still a little shocked by the event that had just happened.

"That is not a bad thing" said the stage four teacher "it is just unusual, as you have never used or experienced these gifts before. In the past you have done everything that everyone has asked of you without thinking. There were no emotions in the past so you just did it without questioning anything but now everything changes. Shall we continue?"

No one answered.

"Ahh, whole class nervousness I see" whispered Mr Church – Hill. "Well not to worry. I am here and I can stop the emotions at any time you want me to but we must continue".

Mr Church – Hill pressed play on the video for the first time, sat down, and began observing the children very closely around his classroom. It made sense that he wasn't paying any attention to the clip, as after all he had seen this video many, many times.

The children had just learned about some of the facts of all three world wars. Why had millions of innocent people suffered pointless deaths? Deaths that were caused by other humans. Deaths that were evil. Deaths that saw really bad people locked up in something called a prison. Mr Church – Hill stopped the video clip about 10 minutes into the lesson. The whole room sat in complete silence, every child now experiencing water drops on their cheeks and water dripping down onto their clothes or even the floor.

Mr Church – Hill stood up slowly and turned the clip off handing out handkerchiefs. "Sadness. Those are tears of sadness rolling down your face. You feel sorry for all those people you have seen in the clips. This is the emotion of crying. That's enough for today children, time to go home".

Next day didn't get any easier. Lasting a bit longer, the children saw more of the tragedies resulting from the world wars on the video clips. Each time Mr Church – Hill showed them more of the video, the children advanced a little further and discovered more about their new gifts of emotions. They had discovered sadness, nervousness and crying. The week had proven difficult for most children. However the pattern of Mr Church – Hill's history lessons continued for the remainder of the year. The children cried a little more each time and a lot more after that, until they started to control their emotions. They had researched starvation, pollution, greed, the extinction of animals and jealousy. It was hard to think that people could be so nasty to each other in the past.

The stage four children had completed their studies for another year but nothing would have a lasting impression more so than these gifts of emotions that had been given.

Millie had understood why these gifts had to be passed on but did think that out of all her time at school, this was probably the most upsetting stage she had been through. She even felt a little sorry for Mr Church – Hill who had to teach the same topic year in year out. However out of all the sad things that Millie had experienced, nothing could prepare her for what happened next. Mr Church – Hill read out a letter that would explain that Daisy Mae's dad had got a job working abroad and that the whole family would be moving with him. The summer holidays and stage five would start without Millie's best friend being there ever again.

Stage five. Mrs Jolly and the gift of …

Mrs Jolly was exactly what she sounded like, chirpy, upbeat, all around positive and full of joy. However Millie was not. She had woken up in the middle of the night being sick.

Millie had been ill once before when she was younger, probably down in stage one, but this time it was completely different. Last time, being sick didn't involve anything else other than letting her body get rid of her stomach contents without any fuss. This time however, the children had now been given the gifts of taste and smell which as you can imagine made the experience very unpleasant. Nevertheless, Millie recovered and was back in school a day later.

Mrs Jolly had explained that the children were going to be expanding their experience and knowledge of emotion further. That night, Mrs Jolly had sent a letter home that needed returning, giving permission for each child to travel to and from events for the next seven weeks. These events could be anything at all and the school would try its best to arrange them if they could. Within a week all permissions were handed in and Mrs Jolly announced that they were ready for their first outing.

Mrs Jolly announced that "this year children we will be encouraging and exploring all the possible emotions. From excitement, passion, fun and laughter to patience, anticipation and appreciation. It really will be a year to remember. Everything will be based on your own passions. I can't wait to see where we end up".

The start of the week saw the class visit a local art gallery where the children were inspired to draw about local features in an under the sea theme. Alexis, Tyler, Lily S and Kiera found this topic exciting and soon realised that they would be blessed with the gifts of patience and attention to detail. Everyone else however, found the topic either boring or so difficult, that they only developed their anger and frustration further. Mrs Jolly did confirm by the end of the week that "not everybody can be good at everything. I think Ashton will be celebrating his eighteenth birthday by the time he finishes his art work".

Week two had a sports theme and naturally Ellis, Robert, Bradley, Dexter, Justin, Natasha, Sophie and Mikey would enjoy these lessons. They excelled in football, winning tournaments for the school while continuing to enjoy and have fun learning to swim. This taught them many skills including the importance of not giving up, trying hard and representing the school badge with pride. In terms of emotion, their hearts had raced up and down as each goal they scored or conceded went in.

Mrs Jolly had a beaming smile when her children had not only been presented with both trophies but heard news that some of her class had made the swim team two years early!

Week three launched an investigation into electricity, exploration, space and all things science. This week would see Archie, Danny, Ethan, George, Brodie and Finley get excited especially when the week finished with a trip to a nearby planetarium. There was excitement and lots of communication as the children developed their emotions further and further.

A unique trip to see the stage six children compete in the football Elliot Cup in week four, allowed the children to explore the build-up of a big match with anticipation and nervousness. Every goal that the stage six children scored allowed the stage five children to jump for joy as their emotions got carried away. TJ never sat in his chair! Mrs Jolly thought that he might explode! The wait for the final whistle was almost like time itself stood still but eventually the game ended and a sense of a well-earned feeling surrounded everyone associated with the school. The Elliot Cup trophy was coming home!

Inside week five the school held its own talent competition with Amelia and Lily C entering. As the duo were about to enter the stage, Amelia asked Mrs Jolly "Why does my tummy hurt?"

The stage five teacher replied "It is what we call butterflies, dear! It happens when you are worried and nervous about performing in front of others especially when it could go wrong". It just so happens that singing and dancing was right up Amelia's and Lily C's street. Once they had got through the opening couple of minutes, their confidence took off so high that you'd think they were born naturals. Chloe T W and Hayley also performed brilliantly with a different kind of act. They had used their excellent skills of imagination and writing in stage three to create their own comedy sketch which made everyone laugh uncontrollably.

In week six the class took a trip to watch Harrison take part in a local BMX bike race. Not only was Harrison daring and courageous, he left is audience on the edge of their seats as he jumped the mud bumps on the curvy, narrow circuit. Mrs Jolly was out of her chair all the time shouting "Go get 'em H. Go and get 'em" or even "Knock him off his bike H, that will teach him a lesson".

Mrs Jolly really was jolly about everything. There was nothing that she wouldn't do for the children in her class.

During week seven, the class built upon their skills of stage two and developed their cooking skills. This was Norman's, Taylor's, Danny's, Chloe B's, Katy's and Millie's favourite week as they had successfully made pizza from start to finish feeling extremely pleased with themselves.

Finley and George weren't as keen at making food as they used to be in stage two, however they still made their pizza successfully. Meanwhile on the other side of the room, there was dough, flour, tomato sauce and cheese all over the place.

"Why are half of your ingredients on your faces Archie and Brodie?" asked Mrs Jolly trying not to laugh at the pair of them. "Well it serves me right. Mr Baker did warn me about the pair of you teaming up. Maybe next time you should have a different partner. One that can help you finish your cooking?" The boys' nodded their heads.

Within an hour of that lesson, Archie and Brodie had redeemed themselves. Mrs Jolly had asked for a write up on how to make a pizza from start to finish and although they hadn't actually made it, they did write down the instructions with the most beautiful handwriting you had ever seen. Then again Mrs Jolly would say that, as she was always in a jolly mood.

Winter would arrive and leave and Mrs Jolly would get on teaching the usual subjects while continuing to expand the children's emotions. This would all gear up for one final trip out at the end of the summer term to a theme park which Hayley and Chloe wrote a poem about.

The whole class took a visit,

to an exciting theme park.

Where we stayed all day,

through until it got dark.

Rollercoasters and log flumes,

and mazes with mirrors.

All before we ate,

Our short but delicious dinner.

Stuffed ourselves with hot
dogs,

From the kiosks that were
scattered around,

Not before going on the big
one,

Getting off and falling to the
ground.

Some coped well, some coped
badly,

Mrs Jolly shouted "Time to go!"

Which upset us all very sadly,

To the coach we must go.

Now was time to go home,

Via the beautiful sea side coast,

Back to our favourite school,

which we love the most.

Mrs Jolly was delighted as usual with their work. She was delighted with everyone in the class.

"Your emotions have been developed children for good and for sad. On top of your speech and listening from stage one, your taste and smell from stage two, your imagination and problem solving from stage three and your dark emotions from stage four, you are now ready to add my jolliness from stage five into your final stage. Stage six!"

Stage Six. Mr Brown and the gift of...

This was it. Millie and the children were only one stage away from receiving their final stage gift.

Millie could remember vividly how when she first started school, the stage six children had stood there speechless. Millie started the usual cycle of questions going around in her head. Did every year group get the same gifts? Maybe each stage gift is different for each class. Maybe it depends on the type of class you are. Millie wasn't sure about anything but one thing for sure was that all the class was ready for their final year. What was their final gift going to be?

Mr Brown was an ordinary, down to earth kind of guy. Up until Christmas, it was a typical routine for the children, as like all other schools there would be exams and tests to see how the children had got on since the start of the new stage.

"Now in the old days" cried Mr Brown, "the children would have to take a test in Maths, English and sometimes Science which might suit some children in the room. However our leaders decided that it wasn't fair on the children who were no good at those types of subjects, so now we let you decide"

"Cool" shouted Ashton.

"Indeed! If you want a P.E test, then we will give you a P.E test and not one that is written work either, one where you can go and play sports all day and pass it very easily. These tests are virtually impossible to fail.

"You mean if I want a dance test all I have to do is dance?" said Amelia.

"Yes!" replied Mr Brown.

Amelia looked excited as did all the other children.

"You have one day to decide what your test will be on and you must let me know by tomorrow. Ok?"

"Ok" everyone answered back.

"I will give you this piece of paper so you can write down your final choice and hand it in to me tomorrow".

Overnight came and went and Mr Brown sat at his desk putting everyone's slip of paper into a bowl ready to be drawn out randomly.

"Each test will be completed on a Friday afternoon. One person each Friday until all thirty children have finished.

"What about Monday to Thursday?" asked Finley.

"We will all practise that person's choice" said Mr Brown grinning.

"You mean if the girls have picked ballet dancing, then we all have to ballet dance for a full week?" asked Justin looking very worried.

"Precisely!" said Mr Brown.

All of a sudden everyone looked a little bit scared. Mr Brown pulled all thirty topics out in a random order.

"Here is the order of our studies. You will need to collect the following books to help us along the way…"

Week 1	The study of Ancient Egypt using the text "You sphinx you know it all?" by Faye O King.
Sophie	
Week 2	The study of computer games by N.O Power.
Ashton	
Week 3	The study of drawing by V. Shady.
Millie	
Week 4	The study of army weapons by Frank Bullet.
Tyler	
Week 5	How to be a face tuber thingy by R. U. Popular.
Archie	
Week 6	Animals in the forest by Theresa Tall.
Natasha	

Week 7 Ellis	How to become a boxer with Mr K.O. Punch.
Week 8 Chloe B	How to dance successfully with Ms. F. "Ace" Plant and Ms Leah Tard.
Week 9 Harrison	A guide to motorbikes with Oi. Lee Chains.
Week 10 Bradley	Are footballers paid enough? By R.U. Joking?
Week 11 Justin	Are footballers really paid enough? By Penny. S. Galore.
Week 12 Mikey	How to make a new vehicle by Ellie Kopter.
Week 13 Taylor	A new gadget that will make millions by Ed Overheels.

Week 14 Danny	Computer games designed by Reverend R.E. Start.
Week 15 Katy	How to write a fantastic novel by Paige Turner.
Week 16 Finley	Ninja sound effects by Master Hiya.
Week 17 Amelia	Animals and their habitats with Bea Keeper.
Week 18 Norman	How to put the ball in the net by Rick O'Shea.
Week 19 Dexter	Why you shouldn't drink and swim by N. O. Water.
Week 20 Alexis	How to follow a wolf by A.Wright Howler.

Week 21 Chloe T W	Horses in the neighbourhood by Mrs Trotsky.
Week 22 Kiera	My two favourite colours are black and
Week 23 Hayley	How to look like a beautiful model by Faye Slift.
Week 24 Lily C	A list of foods that will make you gaseous by Wendy Bottom.
Week 25 Robert	Footballers from 1940 to 1970 by Anne Teak.
Week 26 Brodie	The History of the Titanic by Flo Ting.
Week 27 Lily S	Training of your voice with help from Carol Clarke.

Week 28 Ethan	Electricity by Sir Kit Breaker.
Week 29 T.J.	How not to swim by Flo Tinaway.
Week 30 George	Solids, liquids and gases by Molly Kewell.

All thirty weeks had been completed and all the children had completed everyone's task with lots of laughs and giggles. Millie had tried kicking a football, Harrison tried dancing extremely badly and George got stung by all the bees (which nearly killed him because of all his allergies) but everything turned out fine in the end. Everyone passed their choice of topic and without knowing, the end of the year was upon them.

Mrs Rainbow came into class. "Well children your time here has nearly come to an end. You will be receiving your final gift in the hall tomorrow. Please make sure you are all there for the big occasion".

Millie and all the children had wanted this answer for years and now the day was nearly here. Although everyone was desperate to find out what the final gift was going to be, it was as though nobody wanted to leave or find out what it was. It was going to be hard to say goodbye and leave school for good. There were tears of happiness, something that wasn't possible until two stages ago, great friendships that had developed and been lost (Millie thought about Daisy-Mae) and now everyone was ready to go on to their new stage seven to eleven schools.

Mr Brown said they had been a pleasure to teach and was looking forward to them getting their final stage six gift. He let them go home one last time ready for their final leaver's assembly taking place just after lunch tomorrow.

The morning had begun with the school's usual leavers' rituals of getting each other's shirts signed with lots of messages of good luck from staff and friends. However, time flew and the big moment was here.

The children changed into a fresh set of school uniform clothes and made their way into the hall in front of all the other stages - one final time.

"Good afternoon children" said Mrs Rainbow.

"Good afternoon Mrs Rainbow. Good afternoon everybody" replied the children all except stage one.

"We are here today for our leaver's assembly. Here at the front of the room are the thirty children that will be leaving us this time around. In a moment or two we will be letting our leavers' receive their final stage six gift which I promise you is really something special"

Millie was nearly bursting inside to know what it was. She was so close to finding out.

It was the usual way that each teacher spoke about each child in turn, giving lots of praise. This would go on for a little while and all the children deep inside were thinking hurry up! But time seemed to pass quicker than expected and suddenly Mrs Rainbow spoke again.

"Well children. No time like the present. On your feet please"

Millie stood up as all the stage six children did. She started to feel nervous, anxious and her legs started to shake. Was everyone else feeling the same way? Not everyone could have been she thought. Only children that have been through Mr Church – Hill's and Mrs Jolly's stage would know about emotion.

Mrs Rainbow spoke once more. "Well done stage six children. You have finished your time with us and now is time for you to move on. Take these stage six memories and final gift with you on your journey wherever you may go. I hope it brings you lots of happiness".

Millie closed her eyes and saw herself as that stage one child again. What did all those children get as their final gift each and every year before her?

"Open your eyes Millie" encouraged Mrs Rainbow. Millie opened her eyes and the most astonishing thing in the world had happened.

The gift of...

The whole hall looked on. Millie and all the other leavers stood there in amazement. Every single one of them was speechless, ironically just like they were in stage one. It took a few moments for all the children to gather their thoughts but every one of them that stood at the front of the hall, smiled like all of their Christmas's had arrived at once.

Lily S was the first to try and speak. "But this..."

"Remember Lily, if you say what you shouldn't, you will lose the gift".

In front of each child was every member of the school sitting in the hall. The children, sitting down in stages one to five, had the same puzzled look on their faces that Millie had had five stages ago and the teachers were sitting there with the biggest smiles on their faces ever!

Mrs Rainbow spoke. "Unbelievable? I will walk along the line now and whisper to each child what the name of the gift is that you have received".

Millie was still in shock. She could see Mrs Rainbow getting closer as she moved down the line. What was the name of this gift? How had they managed to keep this a secret every year?

Mrs Rainbow was now at Millie. The head teacher lowered herself and gently spoke the words "Your final gift is the gift of colour!"

Eventually everyone had been spoken to and Mrs Rainbow dismissed the children from stages one to five for the end of the school year.

"Make sure you have one last look around the school and say goodbye to all the teachers before you go. I'm sure you will want to see your school in the real way it has been built with lots of glorious colours and shades".

The first thing the children did was actually look up and down at each other.

"Millie look at George!" said Amelia "What colour is that?"

"Red or ginger hair" replied Miss Bell who was now standing next to them.

Millie and Amelia smiled. George came up to them laughing as well. "What is that colour?" asked George curiously pointing at Amelia's hair.

"Blonde or if you want to learn your first colour: yellow" laughed Mrs Jolly.

This was unbelievable thought Millie. Everywhere she turned to look, everything had a different colour. There were so many colours to look at in so many shades.

"Just you think" said Mr Brown, "everything you have ever done has all been in colour and you never knew. Everything up until this day had been in black and white to you. But as you can see, the world is not black and white and there are so many beautiful things for you to go and explore".

"So that means all the other children see in..."

"Black and white" finished Mr Brown.

"Cool!" shouted TJ.

Millie couldn't wait to explore her new gift. She had already decided that her favourite colour, as described to her by Mr Brown, was pink. However she did agree, just like all the stage six children, that all of the colours were simply beautiful. Life would never be the same again.

Later that evening, Millie climbed into her brown wooden framed bed pulling over her a pink duvet cover. She was admiring a certain very colourful rocket ship that had been made a long, long time ago.

92324398R00059

Made in the USA
Lexington, KY
02 July 2018